This book
belongs to

....

....

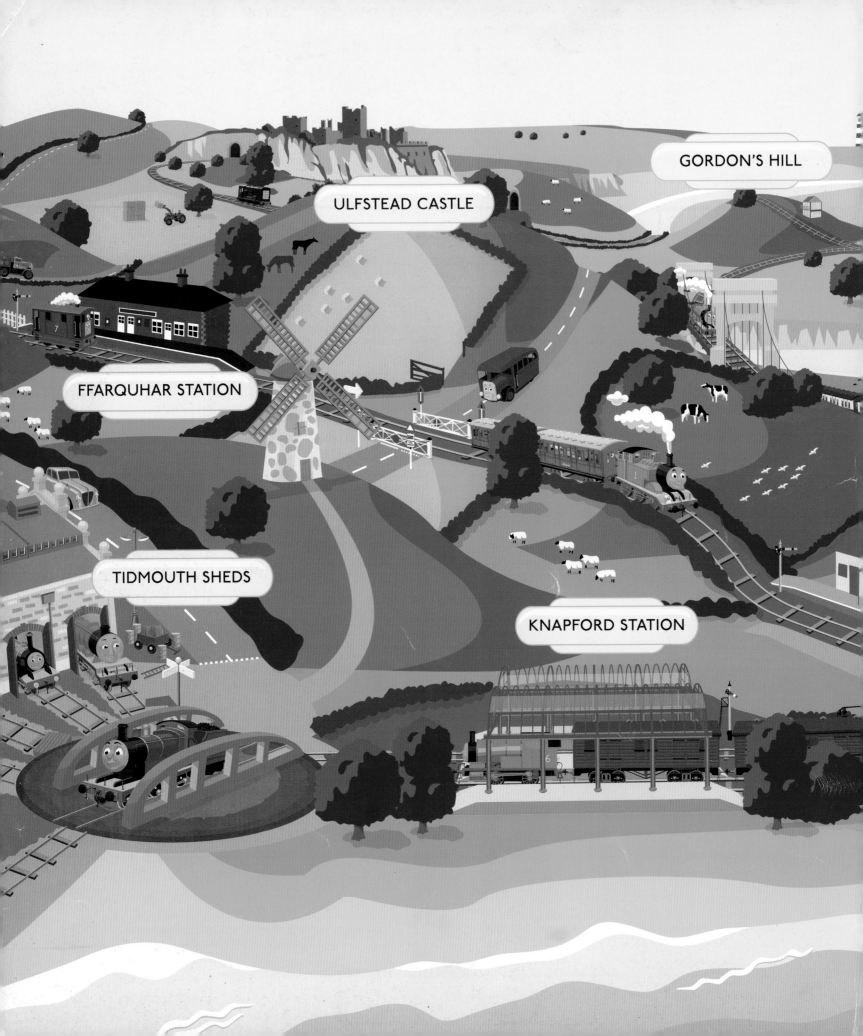

GORDON'S HILL

ULFSTEAD CASTLE

FFARQUHAR STATION

TIDMOUTH SHEDS

KNAPFORD STATION

BRENDAM DOCKS

CHINA CLAY PITS

DRYAW STATION

THE ISLAND OF SODOR

EGMONT
We bring stories to life

First published in Great Britain in 2018 by Egmont UK Limited,
The Yellow Building, 1 Nicholas Road, London W11 4AN

Written by Laura Jackson
Designed by Martin Aggett
Illustrated by Robin Davies
Map illustration by Dan Crisp

 Thomas the Tank Engine & Friends™

HIT entertainment   CREATED BY BRITT ALLCROFT

Based on the Railway Series by the Reverend W Awdry
© 2018 Gullane (Thomas) LLC. Thomas the Tank Engine & Friends and
Thomas & Friends are trademarks of Gullane (Thomas) Limited.
Thomas the Tank Engine & Friends and Design is Reg. U.S. Pat. & Tm. Off.
© 2018 HIT Entertainment Limited.

ISBN 978 1 4052 8923 8
67957/1

Printed in Estonia

Stay safe online. Any website addresses listed in this book are correct
at the time of going to print. However, Egmont is not responsible for content
hosted by third parties. Please be aware that online content can be subject
to change and websites can contain content that is unsuitable for children.
We advise that all children are supervised when using the internet.

Thomas the Tank Engine

A Day at the Football

This is the story about Thomas the Tank Engine and the day he and his friend James got ready for the football match of the season…

It was an exciting day on the Island of Sodor. Sodor United was playing Barrow in the biggest football game of the year.

The Fat Controller arrived at Tidmouth Sheds to give the engines their jobs.

"I'm going to be the referee," he said, proudly. "Thomas and James, I want you to work as a team to get the fans to the football ground at Dryaw."

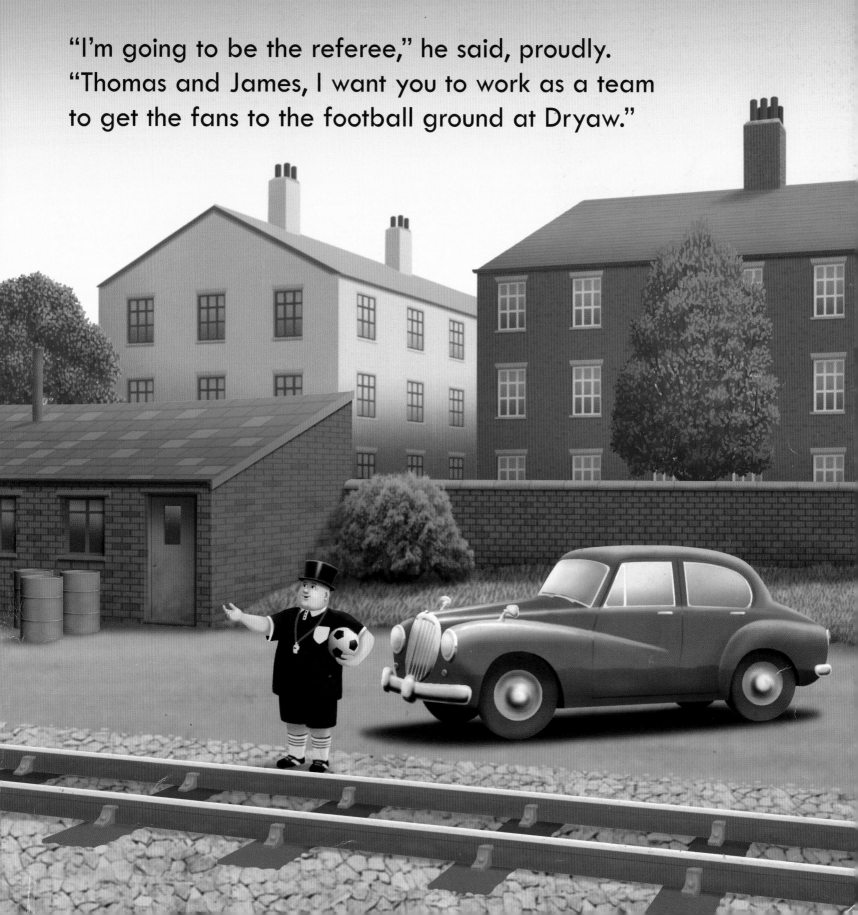

Nobody was more excited than Thomas. Sodor United fans loved Thomas because his blue paint matched Sodor's blue football kit perfectly. Everywhere Thomas went they always gave him the biggest cheer and waved their flags and scarves.

"Go on you blues, Thomas!"

Thomas always felt like he was part of the team.

Poor James was not so excited.
The Sodor fans NEVER cheered for
James because he was painted red.

But today James was in for a big surprise. When he arrived at Brendam Docks, the Barrow fans were all wearing **bright red!** They let out a huge cheer when they saw James' shiny red engine.

"Red en-gine, red en-gine, red en-gine!"

James proudly pulled into Dryaw next to Thomas.
"Look! The Barrow fans are wearing red," puffed James.
"It's **_reds playing blues_** at the football today."

"Who do you think can take their fans to the game the fastest – reds or blues?" Thomas asked, with a smile. **"Let's have a race!"**

James chuffed away quickly and steamed out in front.

Thomas was catching up. **"Too fast, too fast, too fast!"** called out Annie and Clarabel.

Uh oh, red signal! James screeched to a stop.

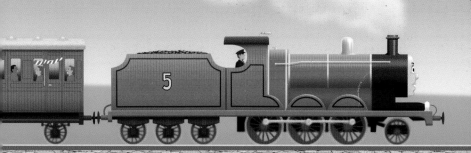

Whirr, whirr, whirr went James' wheels along the track.

Thomas raced on ahead.

"Blues are the best, blues are the best!"

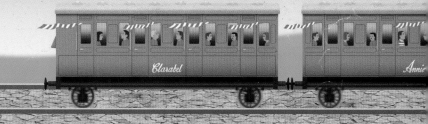

Thomas and James raced around Sodor. Both engines wanted to win so much that they started to make mistakes.

Thomas rushed through the station leaving The Fat Controller on the platform. Thomas was supposed to take him to the game!

"Thomas! Stop!"

And when James arrived at Brendam Docks to collect his last passengers, he was in such a hurry that he pulled away before everyone had climbed aboard. He didn't realise that his last passengers were the Barrow football team!

"No! James, come back!"

Thomas and James had no idea the trouble they had caused as they screeched to a stop at the pitch.

Thomas and James both thought they had won the race, but soon realised the game had not started. The Fat Controller arrived with the Barrow football team. He was very cross!

"You were meant to work together today, not against each other," he said. "I'm giving you a yellow card as a warning. If you cause any more trouble you will be given a red card and you won't be allowed to watch the match!"

Thomas and James felt terrible. They had nearly ruined the biggest football match of the year. Suddenly the fans began booing. "The trophy is missing!" cried The Fat Controller. "I don't know where I left it."

"James, if we work together we can find the trophy and be back before the game is over," said Thomas. This time they were determined to show The Fat Controller that they were a Really Useful team.

Thomas raced to the Docks where The Fat Controller had been to greet some fans. No trophy there.

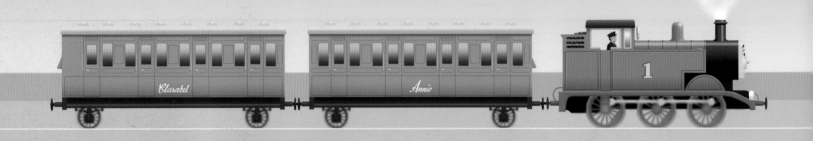

Thomas headed to the sports shop where The Fat Controller had been to pick up a new whistle. The trophy was nowhere to be found.

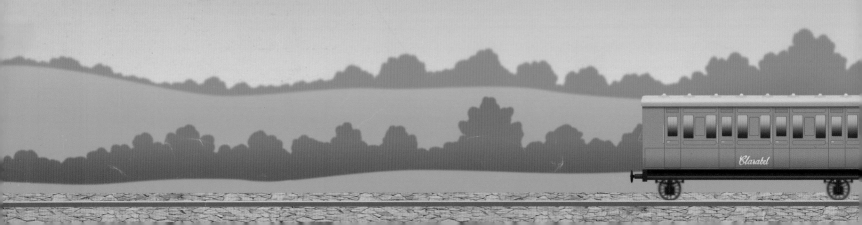

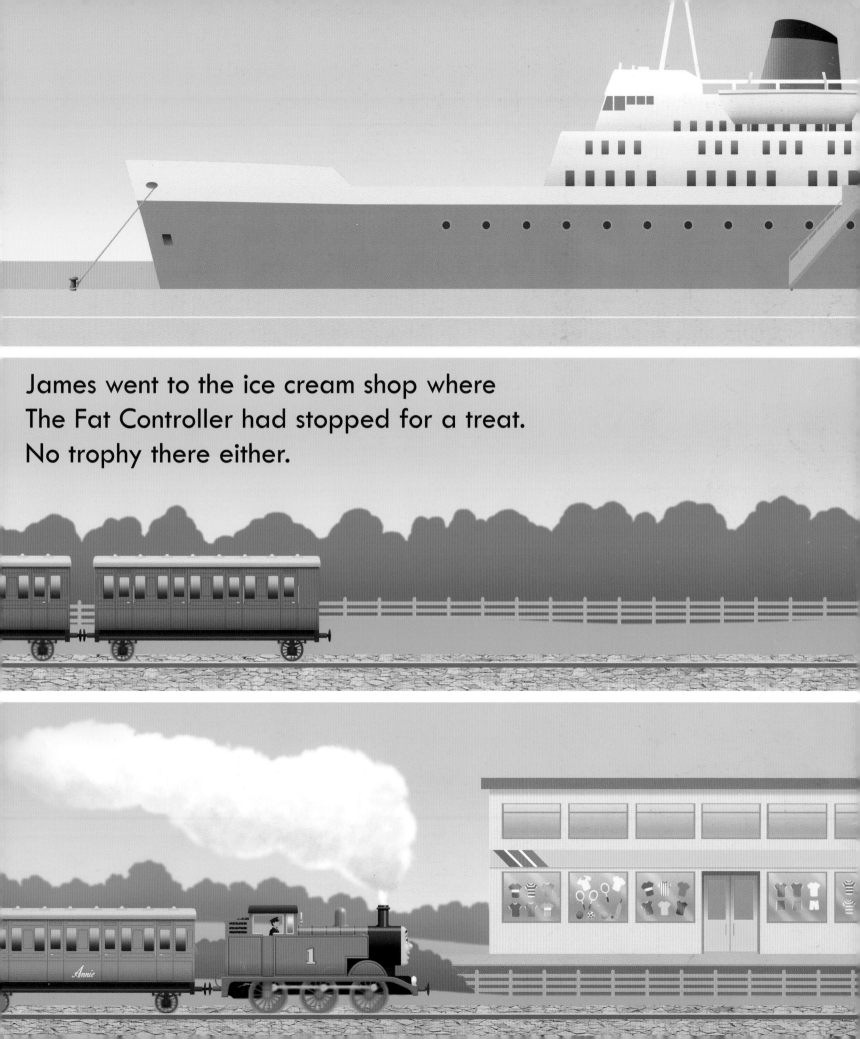

James went to the ice cream shop where
The Fat Controller had stopped for a treat.
No trophy there either.

Finally, James screeched into Kellsthorpe Station. He had spotted the trophy on the platform.

"Quick! I need to get back to the football game," James shouted. The trophy was loaded into James' carriage and he raced as fast as he could back to Dryaw.

Thomas was waiting. They had arrived just in time to catch the end of the match.

The fans all cheered the two engines who had saved the day.

"Well done, engines!" cheered The Fat Controller. "You make a great team." Just then, the football shot off the pitch and landed with a pop – right in Thomas' funnel!

The two friends laughed as Thomas blew the football out of his funnel and straight into the goal.

"Goooooooooal!"

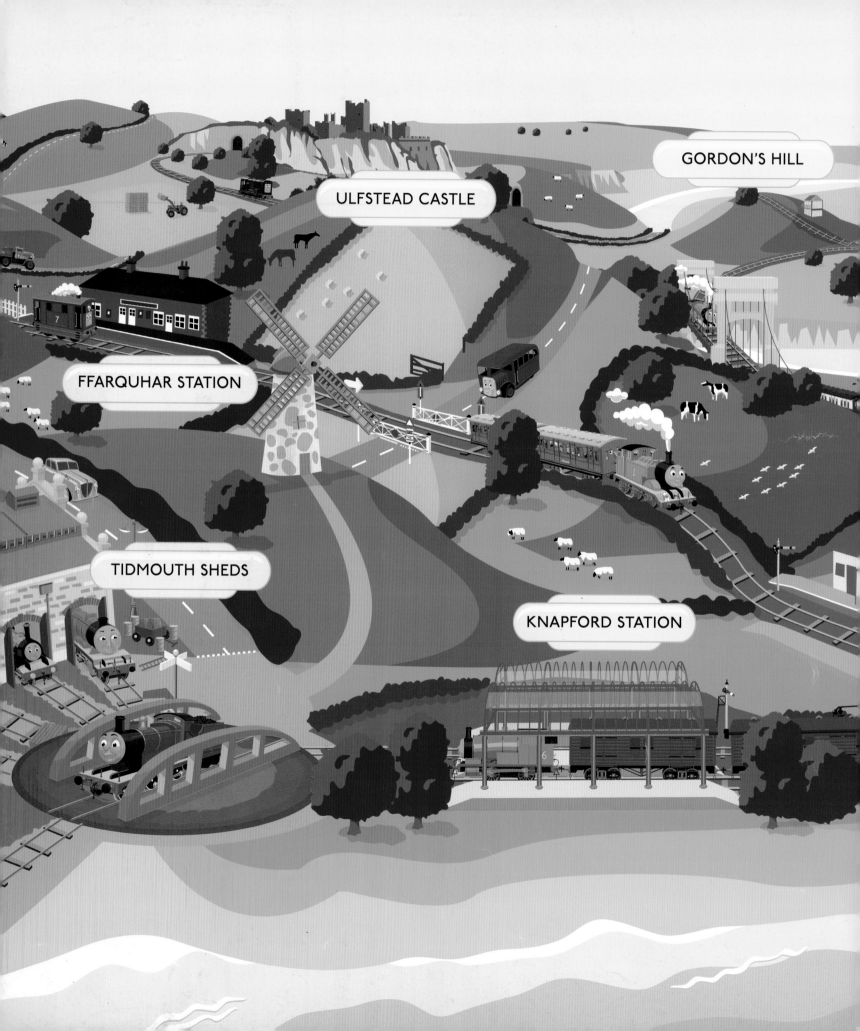

GORDON'S HILL

ULFSTEAD CASTLE

FFARQUHAR STATION

TIDMOUTH SHEDS

KNAPFORD STATION

BRENDAM DOCKS

CHINA CLAY PITS

DRYAW STATION

THE ISLAND OF SODOR

The Reverend W. Awdry was the creator of 26 little books about Thomas and his famous engine friends, the first being published in 1945. The stories came about when the Reverend's two-year-old son Christopher was ill in bed with the measles. Awdry invented stories to amuse him, which Christopher then asked to hear time and time again. And now for over 70 years, children all around the world have been asking to hear these stories about Thomas, Edward, Gordon, James and the many other Really Useful Engines.

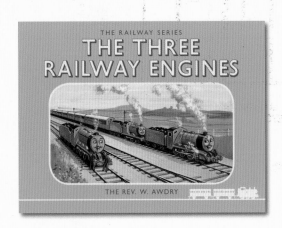

The Three Railway Engines, first published in 1945.

The Reverend Awdry with some of his readers at a model railway exhibition.